KNIGHTS OF THE IMMORTALS

KNIGHT'S APPRENTICE

BY CATRINA TAYLOR

Knights of the Immortals
The Knight's Apprentice

Written by Catrina Taylor
Cover art on digital version created by Sami Miko
Cover Design by The Writing Network

MidnightRose
Copyright 2015,2016
ISBN 978 1 63310 031 2

Thank you in advance for your review.

Dedication

This series is dedicated to the incredible people who inspired the stories, my children, nieces and nephews. It's dedicated to the readers who have helped to breathe life into all of my stories. Without you, there would be no knights.

My thanks for every part of this goes to the incredible team that helped with the development - Karyn Pearson, my relentless editor and dearest friend; Sami Miko, the talented artist; 'Kick' my niece who visually recreated our beloved apprentice; KG Stutts, my incredible friend, beta reader and support. Without you, this series would still be a figment of my imagination. Thank you.

Other Books By Catrina Taylor

Xarrok Novels
Birth of an Empire Series
    The Beginning
    Consequences
    Homecoming
    The Fall

Xarrok Origin Stories
    By Flame
    Through Anguish
    Mind Tricks
    Below the Surface
    Change by Design

Xarrok Saga One through Five

Knights of the Immortals
    Knight's Apprentice
    The Choosing

KNIGHT'S APPRENTICE

Prologue

"Every ounce of life felt, falls back to the surface it began from. With this stroke, let it be, that his last breath is known to me." With a quiet force, the knight's sword bears down upon a man. A crack, a gasp, and a final exhale follow. The aged man withdraws the sword and kneels beside the body. "It is done, old friend. May you find peace."

The man lifts his arm to reach for the knight, and the light of the moon reflects in his eyes. A hint of a smile tells the knight his duty is complete. Fleeting traces of life expire with the final breath, leaving the knight alone with his thoughts.

A moment spent in silent remembrance is interrupted. A twig cracks in the clearing. The old man turns his head and removes his helmet to get a better look. He peers through the tree line to find the motion forcing his focused attention. The shape of a person falls back into the shadows, and he moves toward it with a speed unnatural for his age and armor.

Crossing the tree line, he finds a young woman frantically trying to pick up groceries. Her dark ponytail has started to fall, and the swiftness of her movements indicates fear. He kneels next to her, begins picking up cans, and hands them to her. He continues without a word.

His hands move faster than hers to collect several items at a time and deposit them either in her grasp or bag. When she finally acknowledges him, her face pales and her lips quiver.

"Please, don't hurt me. I won't tell a soul. Promise." Her voice is panic stricken

The knight tilts his head. "Hurt you? Why would I do that?"

With wide eyes she looks at the body in the field. "You . . ."

A smile purses his expression as he realizes what caused her fear. "You believe I killed him?"

"I . . . um . . . yes."

"He was one of my oldest friends. I couldn't bring harm to him no matter what came over me." The knight stands at his full height and extends a hand to the girl. "You're safe. Did you recover everything?"

Her eyes drop to the ground around her again, searching for what might be left. "I . . . I think so.

"Good." He glances over his shoulder and hears a whisper. He knits his brow as he responds. "She's among the humans. She wouldn't understand."

The girl begins to turn away, but hears his response, causing her to pause.

The whisper urges him again.

He responds to it, "I was planning to return home after this task to find someone better qualified."

Finally speaking up, the girl asks, "What are you talking about? Better qualified for what? Won't understand what?" She hesitantly looks at him.

He sighs heavily. "Come." He extends his hand to carry her bag, but when she clutches it to her, he gestures toward the field again.

She follows slowly behind him. Her arms keep the grocery bag close, and her bookbag remains on her back.

He guides her across the field to the body of his dear friend. He pulls the sword from the ground next to him and tilts it halfway. Placing a hand beneath the lower point of the hilt, two small round objects drop. "These are markers. It will send notice to his people that he is ready for burial. His body will be placed among those of his forefathers."

He kneels over the man placing one of the round objects on his head and the other at his feet. A moment later, a dull light shimmers around the body and it vanishes.

The girl gasps.

"You . . . He?" She takes a deep breath. "He's alien?"

"No, actually he's of Earth. He was born here a couple centuries ago. His name was Jasper VanDernal. He was a friend from my apprenticeship and beyond." The knight drops his eyes to where his friend had been. "He contracted an illness that was torturing him. He came to me to request I help him find dignity. The council approved the request and the Vampyric Rite of Peace was performed." His eyes lift to meet her open jawed expression. "That's what you witnessed. His passing with peace and dignity."

"He's . . . he was . . ." She takes a deep breath before she asserts, "No. Vampyres are a thing of myth." She spins on her heel and starts across the field again. "There's no way."

The knight chuckles. "I told you she wouldn't understand."

The whispering continues in his ear.

"Are you joking? The sword only works for those who would become knights. It was designed that way. Even if she is of our kind, she's too old to begin now, and you are expecting a lot from a child of this world instead of our own."

The whispers urge him forward.

He closes his eyes and sighs. "As you wish." With uncanny speed, he catches her once again. "May I ask you a favor please?"

Her eyes narrow slightly. "What?"

"Would you hold this for me?" He extends the hilt of the sword to her.

"My hands are full."

"It is something that would only take a moment, and I can hold the groceries for you."

"First, tell me who you've been talking to."

"You're rather demanding for a young one."

The whisper commands him to tell her.

"I was speaking with the grand council." He shifts weight between his feet.

"Council of what?" Her voice is terse.

"Immortals." Without giving her time to absorb the information, he takes the groceries from her hand. "I'm being urged to test your viability and thus, it would be helpful to end this long evening if you would please hold onto the hilt of the sword."

"Fine." She snatches the sword from him and her arm drops slightly. "There. Now can I have my groceries back?"

"Of course." Before his hand makes contact with the sword again, his armor begins to retract and he freezes. Each section folds within the one before it, gradually exposing his human form. "By all that I have seen . . ."

A slight glow emanates from the hilt. Boots fold from her toes up to her knee, and from her knee to the hip, another metal part extends. Soon her legs are fully encompassed by the armor. It continues up her abdomen, onto her chest, arms, and finally over her head. Once she stands fully clad in a shiny armored shell, she drops the sword. "What did you do to me?"

"Nothing. It seems the council is correct. You are Atlantean."

Knight's Apprentice

Chapter 1

Cerita yawns when her alarm goes off. Her hand slaps down on the white clock radio her mother purchased as a gift when she entered high school. The blaring noise is silenced for a few more minutes, and she rolls over, hugging the blankets. It is her every intention to savour the next few precious moments of sleep before her long day begins again.

First she will get her shower, then she will wash her baby sister. While her brothers get ready for school, Mom will feed Carolina, and she will get a smoothie before taking the youngest two to daycare on her way into school herself. She is thankful every day that her brother, Carlos is able to get himself to the bus. It was one less thing for her already hectic morning.

Her mom would walk half a mile to the hotel today, so she can take the family car to school and get to work afterward. Today will be an easy day for her at work. She only has four hours and can spend part of it doing her homework, but she isn't getting out of bed until the snoozed alarm forces her to.

Before she wants it to, the day finally begins. She forces herself, in her exhausted state of mind, out into the hallway and chaos of the family morning. Before long, she loads her brother and sister in the brown, rusty, four-door blessing they call the family car. Once she drops them off, she makes her way to school, which is only a few blocks from the daycare center. She'll return to later to bring her youngest siblings to Carlos at home on her way to work.

When she parks in the student parking lot, she searches for her bookbag and realizes she has the diaper bag instead. With a frustrated sigh, she pulls out and heads back to the daycare center to exchange the bags. "Leave it to me to be late to school when I've got two major tests."

She meanders through the day, moving from one class to the next, still exhausted and haunted by the strange dream she had the night before. She actively takes notes in every class and prepares herself for the exams when she's able. By lunch she begins to wake. She brings her notebooks and tray outside to the grass where Jenna is already settled. Best friends since middle school, and she's still not sure if she wants to tell her about this strange dream. "You ready for the test?"

Jenna looks up at her, tucking a blonde lock behind her ear. "In Sosh? Yep. I think I memorized everything Napoleon did in the last two combat situations. You?"

"Yeah. I think that's going to be the easy exam today." She settles down and stretches out. "The science test with Mr. Derivan is going to be far more challenging."

"At least he likes you. He'll go easy on you with it."

"He likes the fact I'm nice to him when he comes to the hotel with his kids." She picks up her sandwich and cracks open her notebook. Her eyes rest on the page but she's unable to focus enough to study. The words begin to merge. She lifts her eyes from her notes. Allowing her gaze to drift to the fields and tables watching as students move about the campus, her mind also wanders. "You ever have one of those dreams that are so real and vivid that you feel like it actually happened? Even to the point of exhaustion?"

"I can't say I've been tired from a dream but I know the real feel kind." Jenna lifts her head from the books. "What's up?"

"I don't know. I thought I saw some old man kill another one, but then it turned out I saw some space thingy, and I was told that I'm from Atlantis." She shakes her head. "I don't know. It was just really strange."

Jenna's soft blue eyes fix on her friend. "You had this last night?"

"Yep. So real, I'm not sure it was a dream. I mean I am, because that's so . . . but still, it was just that real." Cerita turns away from Jenna, dropping her eyes to the tray to grab the apple. "Strange, huh?"

"Yep. Strange." Jenna opens a book next to her. "We should make sure we've got science down."

"Right. That test is nearly half our grade this quarter."

Over the rest of their lunch period, they both prepare for their science exam. When they enter the last class of the day and settle into their seats, Cerita finds her mind drifting again. A hand taps her shoulder and she jumps in her chair, nudging the desk and drawing attention to herself.

A deep voice apologizes, "Sorry, Cerita. Didn't mean to scare ya."

She calms her breathing and looks toward James. His deep eyes always keep her attention, but the warmth of her cheeks remind her she's not getting lost in them this time. "You didn't. I was spacing. What's up?"

"Do you have an extra pencil? I may have broken mine on my lit exam last class." His eyes never leave hers.

"Oh, um . . . yeah, I should have one." She quickly rummages through the pockets in her bookbag and pulls out a freshly sharpened pencil. "Here."

When he takes the pencil, he holds her hand a moment longer than necessary. "Thank you."

Jenna giggles in the chair next to her.

Both of them look at her and withdraw from their interaction.

The teacher enters the room, hands them the exam, and the room becomes silent. Each student focuses intently on the page ahead of them. The only sounds heard are pencils scratching on paper and pages being flipped one at a time, until each test is complete.

Sounds of desks and chairs screeching across the floor are heard when the exams are turned in. One by one, the room slowly empties.

Through it all, Cerita has to redirect her wandering mind. The final minutes of the class tick down, and she finds herself paying more attention to the clicking of the second hand than to the last few questions on the page before her.

Finally, the teacher's hand reaches for the page and takes it from her. Her eyes drift up to his face, knowing the disappointment in the teacher's expression better than she wants to. When he turns from her desk to his own, she collects her things and moves slowly out of the class.

Jenna rests against the wall outside of the room. "Well? How do you think you did?"

She shrugs. "I don't know. I didn't finish."

"That's never good in Mr. Derivan's class." Jenna put her hand on her friend's arm. "Come on. Let's get your brother and sister and get to work."

"Right. Better things to think about." Cerita walks with her friend out to the parking lot. Her shoulders curl inward the closer they get to the car. She mumbles, "I should never have let that get to me. Not today of all days." She yawns.

"Don't stress. You've got great grades. Things are going to be just fine."

"Yeah, but I'm not looking forward to explaining this to Mom. I need college or we're not . . ." She sighs again. "Let's just get going. Carlos should be home any moment."

"Alright. But you might want to talk to him first." Her head gestures to James, who is leaning on Cerita's car. "Been waiting long?"

A slight perk to one cheek betrays his uncertainty. "Not really."

Cerita stops short, her heart throbs loudly in her ears, as it always does when she's near him. "Hi."

His focus falls to her. "Hi." There is a long pause before he says, "Right, uh, Friday I've got plans to see *Cybernetic Galaxy*. I was, um . . . wondering. Would you want to come?"

Cerita tucks an imaginary strand of hair behind her ear. Her cheeks feel warm. "I can't. I have to work. It's my long shift at the hotel."

"Oh? You work at a hotel?" James shifts his

weight.

"Yes. We're taking my baby brother and sister to my other brother 'til Mom gets off. Jenna and I work together."

"That's cool." He smiles. "You get a dinner break right?"

Cerita drops her eyes, not sure what she should say.

"Yes, she gets a break. Come by around nine. It's the large bed and breakfast off the highway. Thomson's Inn. Bring food for the crew." Jenna winks.

James chuckles. "Hope pizza is good."

"Yep. I love pizza. Anything but anchovies. Never got why people want fish on pizza." Jenna opens the door and settles into the passenger seat of Cerita's car. "See you tomorrow night."

Cerita rolls her eyes and sits in the driver's seat. "You don't have to if you don't want to."

James leans over the driver's side door and holds her gaze. "I want to. If it's the best way to see you outside of school, I'm looking forward to it. A lot."

She swallows hard. "Right." A broad smile lightens the moment. "See you tomorrow night."

The girls pull away and Cerita turns her focus to her friend. "I can't believe you did that."

"Did what? The two of you have been playing cat and mouse for almost a year now. He finally got the nerve to be direct about it, and you were going to blow him off." Jenna tilts her head toward her. "A good friend wouldn't let a friend ignore the boy she's crushing on."

Cerita laughs. "Right. Whatever."

The ride to the daycare is short, and between the two friends, the kids are quickly strapped in their seats without incident. After swinging by Cerita's house to bring Carolina and Ciro to Carlos, they head to work for the night. The evening is uneventful, and as it draws to a close, they begin packing their bags. "You started the audit reports for tomorrow morning?"

Jenna lifts her hands from the keyboard. "Yep, and I scheduled check out records for the boss lady too. Gave her a bonus. I prepped her paperwork for housekeeping in the morning."

"You're on the ball tonight."

She laughs. "Have to be, you've been distracted all day."

Cerita winces. "I'm sure after a good night's sleep I'll be fine."

"Yep. Me too." Jenna smiles, throws her bag over her shoulder and clocks out. "Come on, great distracted one. It's eight and we're off."

Cerita clocks out, grabs the keys to the car, and heads to the front to lock the doors for the night. When the system accepts her code she turns to Jenna. "We're good here." Together, they move to the car and drop their bags in the back seat. "You sure about having company at work tomorrow?"

"You've watched your brother and sister at

the hotel before. I'm sure the boss lady will be fine with James bringing us a late meal. Not only that, but she knows all about how you two never seem to get together." She grins.

"Ugh. You and your big mouth." Cerita pulls the car out of the lot, turns onto the main road, and slams on the brakes. Her eyes grow big, and her breathing becomes labored. "Do you see that?"

"See what?"

"That!" Cerita points to a light that starts to dim.

Jenna glances in the direction indicated and closes her eyes. "Yep. Drive. We're on a deadline to get home, remember?"

"But -"

"Go. It's not affecting us, and traffic is backing up."

Cerita's brow knits. "Why are you so calm? That's the guy from the strange dream I had. He's . . . he's suited again. Armored again. His looks dingier than mine did, but gah! This has to be a dream. There's no way I was really wearing armor that put itself on, or . . . ugh!"

Jenna looks over her shoulder. "The light is green. Go."

Cerita screeches into the next parking lot, and into a space near the source of the light. Climbing out of the car, she runs toward where she saw the light begin, and sure enough, the man is standing there. "What? You're real?"

The man chuckles. "Yes, Cerita. I'm real."

"I thought it was a dream."

Jenna runs up to her. "Come on. I'm going to be late. Mom will kill me if we get home late again."

Cerita points to the armored man. "But . . . he's the guy . . ."

"Yeah, yeah, you're somehow of Atlantis. Right. I remember." Jenna turns to the knight. "Did she actually get covered in armor?"

He nods.

Jenna turns to Cerita. "You're of knight's blood." She shrugs and turns back toward the car. "Let's go."

"Cerita, you should head home. I never like it when her kind is unhappy with their young."

Cerita looks at her friend, and back to the knight. "Her kind?"

He smiles, extends a hand, and steps into another light source that blinks out when he is no longer in view.

"Ugh." Cerita stomps back to the car. Once she pulls out into traffic she asks, "What did he mean by your kind?"

"Why didn't you tell me you were covered in armor at lunch?"

"I thought it was a strange dream. I didn't believe it was real. What does it matter anyway?"

"It matters. A lot." Jenna closes her eyes and takes a deep breath. When she opens them her arms are fur covered, and her hands have long claws at the end. "Some of us know about Atlantis. But most of us who do aren't homo-sapiens."

Cerita rolls her eyes and briefly takes her eyes off the road to glance at her friend. Her voice catches in her throat. "What . . . the . . .?"

"Advanced microbot tech allows me to maintain a homo-sapien form. Mom and Dad got tired of Atlantis while I was young, so we moved where we have family on the main land. Here. We all had to have the tech installed to pass through." Jenna sighs and brings back the form her friend has become used to. "If you were able to activate a Knight's Sword, you are of the homo-supreme bloodline in a knight's DNA pool."

"What are you talking about?" Cerita tries to remain focused on the road. The sound of cars passing her seem distant. "You . . . I mean this is . . . ugh! We've been best friends since we were in sixth grade. What else didn't you share . . . why should I . . . ah!"

"Breathe, Cerita." Jenna reminds her of the turn, and the car makes it down to the end of the road leading to her home. "You have had a rough two nights. Mind answering a few questions before I head in?"

Cerita parks the car in her friend's driveway. "What?"

"How'd you happen upon the knight?"

"I was walking home last night after stopping by the store when we got off work. I had an arm full and he killed a man."

"Was it a battle?"

"No."

"Then he was performing a rite. At least, that's the most likely. He won't kill unless someone is a threat. It's part of a knight's creed."

"Why do you know so much?"

"Like I said, I lived in Atlantis. You have no idea how hard it is to avoid telling people the stories are history instead of myth." Jenna crosses her arms. "My brother wanted to be a knight. He did a lot of research. He did activate a wercat knight's sword but mom wouldn't let him go off-world to train so, he's still here."

"Your brother is nine."

"Yep. I doubt you'd be recruited because knights need to start young."

"Wait. Why would . . ." She presses her lips together. "I'll ask mom when I'm home."

"Well, you know my secret. Don't share it."

"Why would I? Who'd believe me anyway? They'd lock me in the loony bin for crazy statements like, 'my best friend is a wercat' or 'some old man told me I'm from a mythological city on the bottom of the sea.'"

Jenna giggles. "Good point. You're taking all of this well."

"I don't have time to be crazy. Mom and the kids need me."

"Yeah, I guess they do. If you ever want to see the city sometime, let me know. I'll talk Mom into it."

"I don't see that happening. Nothing about life has changed for me, and it won't."

Jenna shrugs. "If you say so. You're the first and only homo-supreme I know not in Atlantis. Believe me, life's changed a lot knowing my best friend is like me."

"Like you?" The confused expression on Cerita's face must speak volumes because Jenna changes position.

"You still don't know, I guess. Homo-supreme don't need the micobots like a few of us hominids that appear more animal like. However, you have a lot of options available that others couldn't imagine. You'll live a much longer life than homo-sapiens. You're faster than you realize, but then you're not much of a sports person. You've got other advantages too, but having babies won't be one of them. We don't have many kids if we aren't in Atlantis. The hominids that needed to take refuge there all faced the same common issue. We don't have the ability to procreate often. That's why Mom's got two of us so far apart. It takes a lot more than for others." Jenna pauses. "Your mom's homo-sapien. Your homo-supreme genes come from your dad."

"Why do you say that?"

"There are four of you, and two clustered sets. Not how we have them. Some do, but it's not normal. When did your dad disappear?"

"There was a car accident. When he came

around he didn't remember us. A few days out of
his coma, he left the hospital and we've never
seen him since."

"That was ten years ago, right?"

"Yeah. I miss him every day. Mom keeps
looking out for him, hoping and praying for him,
but he never comes home. We've never seen
him." Her eyes drop to her lap.

Jenna hugs her best friend. "There's no way
to verify my hunch, but it fits fifth grade science
where I'm from." There's a brief pause. "You'll be
fine. I'm not going anywhere."

Cerita holds her friend tightly. "Thanks."

"Jenna. Jenna, you need to come in." The
voice of her mother carries into the car. "Cerita
has a guest."

The girls release their embrace in surprise,
and both turn toward the porch. Beside the long
blonde haired woman on the porch is an older
man with thick silver streaks intertwined with
his patches of dark locks. His stature is taller than
Jenna's mother, but far from tall. His shoulders
are wide, and his form is clearly in shape for a
man of any age, regardless of what his other
features indicate. The girls exchange looks and
both get out of the car.

As they step onto the top stair, the man
greets them in a familiar voice. "Hello, Cerita.
Jenna."

Neither responds before entering the living
room.

Jenna's mom settles in the main chair. "Your dad is still out handling some clan business. He'll be home late."

"Okay." Jenna sits on the couch next to her friend.

Cerita looks at the older man. "Why do you keep following me?"

"I do not 'keep following you.' Earlier, I was near other business. After speaking with the council and seeing you two together, I determined this was a safe place to talk." He tucks his hands into his blue jeans. "The council would like me to bring you to Atlantis. They want to name you my apprentice."

"Your what?"

Jenna grabs her friend's hand. "Isn't she too old to be an apprentice?"

He nods. "That's what I asked the council. They insist I need one, and they are more insistent that she's the person I pick. I was expecting to be home within the month to pick someone, but after our encounter last night . . . well, I'm here."

"No. I will not." Cerita folds her arms across her chest. "I'm not changing my life. Mom is content where we are, and this is what it is."

"I thought you'd say that. I explained you're raised among these people and that it's a good idea not to disrupt your life. The council still begs to differ and offered something for your training."

"I'm not interested, mister."

"It's Ralph. I'm Ralph Fredrickson. You may address me as Master Knight once we begin." He holds his hand out to Jenna's mother. "You have the device?"

The woman extends a small cube toward the knight. "Of course."

He takes it from the wercat and runs his hand over the top without making contact. Above it shines a projection of her earlier day. "This is your everyday routine. The council intends to move things in such a way to allow this routine to become easier on your family as a whole. Also, they are offering to look deeper into the disappearance of your father."

She gasps. "How did you know about that?"

"I didn't. The council found it, and has begun work on the unique situation. It's rare one of our own disappears like that. It's in the best interest of all involved if the council researches the information." Mr. Fredrickson pulls up an image of her father exiting the main hospital doors. "This is the last information provided."

Cerita's eyes tear up instantly. Her throat dries. When she speaks, her voice is soft and strained. "Daddy . . ."

"They can find him, given enough time. They will work on it if you're training or not, but it would be good for you to be training." He clears his throat. "Call it thanks."

"Can I think about it?" It's all the effort

Cerita can give to force out, "Please."

"Of course." He crosses to where she's seated and kneels. "I want to give this to you." He extends a small dagger toward her. The hilt is about the size of her hand, and the blade extends a few inches longer than the hilt itself. "It's from Atlantis, and it was sent for you. The council requested you be gifted this for two reasons. One, as you learn more about the world as it really is instead of as you've known it, you will find dangers will seek you. Two, it will enable you to make contact with other Atlanteans, myself included."

She takes the dagger and looks over it closely. "Thank you. I should go,"

Almost numb, she makes her way back to the car and finds herself parking at home before she is aware of her own thoughts again. She tucks the dagger into her backpack, and slings it over her shoulder before entering the house. Her mother is at the table with a hot cup of coffee. "Everything okay, Mama?"

Her mother looks up and shakes her head. Tears well in her aged features. "No, mi hija."

She settles at the table, across from Carmen. "What happened?"

"The hotel is closing. They laid off everyone except management and two others to maintain the basics until the final closing." Her hands tremble as she lifts the coffee to her lips. "I'm so sorry."

Cerita extends a hand to her mother's arm. "Nothing for you to be sorry for. Mama, we'll be fine. I'll pick up extra hours at the Inn and you'll find another job, I'm sure. We'll be fine."

"I don't know about that this time. With the surgery, your school, and the kids, we . . ." Tears fall as her mother forces another sip of the coffee. "Don't worry yourself with this. You should rest. You have a long day tomorrow."

Chapter 2

The morning greets her like any other. Her mind wanders through her routine with little acknowledgment. She doesn't take Carolina or Ciro to daycare so her mother can spend time with them before finding new work. She avoids Carlos when he begs her for a ride to school, but finds herself pulling into the middle school nonetheless.

Before hopping out of the car, Carlos turns to Cerita. "You okay? You don't look so good."

She blinks then allows her eyes to drift in his direction. "Yeah. Just have a lot on my mind."

"Like Mom's job?"

"Among other things, yes."

"Look, we've been good since Dad left. Even when Mom had that jerk around for a while and he left behind Carol and Ciro like an idiot, we've been fine. We've got this. Really. That's what family is. We stick together, right?"

A half smile lifts her cheeks. "Right."

He spins in the chair and slides from the car. "Catch ya at home. Later."

She watches him head to a group of friends before pulling out of the parking lot, wishing she could share an inkling of what she is consumed with. Even if she did share, who would she share with? Who would believe her? Her whole life just became one big fairy tale full of chaos. Something the Grimm brothers might have been happy to have created.

Without realizing it, she pulls into the high school parking lot and finds her belongings. As she zips up the bookbag, Jenna drops her head in the driver's side window.

"So . . . ready for an easy day?"

Cerita jerks when her friend starts talking. "Don't scare me like that. Ugh."

"Oops."

"I think I'm skipping the last few periods to spend time in the art hall today." Cerita opens the door and slides out. "I've got to work out some things and after those exams, I know I can't look Mr. Derivan in the face today."

"Want company?"

"No. I think this stuff calls for some solo time." She follows Jenna into the school like every other day before it. Nothing really feels different from how it was a few days before, yet her whole world has been knocked on its ear.

"Yep, I get that." After a brief stop at their lockers, Jenna reminds her, "Don't forget you need that clear mind for your dinner tonight." She winks and heads to her homeroom across the school.

Cerita almost laughs at the thought of something so normal as she wanders through the crowd, to her homeroom, so she can check in.

The school day passes as any other day. Her Friday mercy includes a weekend without homework. Although Jenna rambles on about their day on the way to work, it comes without interruption or acknowledgment.

It only takes a few minutes to shift change with the owners of the inn. Cerita reviews expected arrivals and meal orders. She prepares the list for the kitchen staff and prints it for their evening routine. While she begins applying the meal costs to each of the evening orders, Jenna stops her.

"What's going on? You're not talking to me."

"Huh? Sorry. I hadn't noticed. Trying to work on this early. Just want it done before company comes."

Jenna's eyes narrow. "Are you nervous about tonight?"

Cerita shrugs and continues working.

"If that's what it is, you know he's been crushin' on you for ages now. At least as long as you've been crushin' on him. I know it's going to be great tonight."

Cerita's eyes half look toward her friend, half remain on the screen. "Oh. That's not it."

"Are you joking?" Her voice is dry, and her hands input the codes for the next customer's room. "Look, if you need help with this, I can help."

Cerita places a hand on her hip, turns to her friend, and everything on her mind bubbles over at once, "Look, Jenna, I know you think you've got a clue about all this stuff, but you really don't. You haven't spent your whole life thinking you're one thing, only to find out you're something you don't even know a thing about.

"You haven't had to watch your mom desperate to provide for four children and herself. Then watch her lose her job because she's not management when layoffs start. You've not measured the food to make sure everyone else gets enough to eat. Meanwhile you heap your plate full at lunch, because some days school is the only way to get a meal. You haven't had to come home to find your mom in tears because we shut off something other people think is crucial.

"At this point I should be looking at colleges. We only have two years to pick, but I can't. I have to find a way to help Mom, and my kid brothers, and sister. So, if I seem a little disconnected tonight, I've got a lot on my mind. And James is really not that important right now."

Jenna hangs her head and turns her focus to

her terminal. A customer comes in, she checks them in with a smile, and walks them to their room. When she gets back to the front desk to find another one checked in and two more in line. She waits quietly while Cerita does the registration paperwork. Jenna walks the new guests to their rooms. This routine continues for a few hours.

Although the shared work is not uncommon with them, the silence between them is. Jenna's eyes dart to the clock just after eight. She takes Cerita's hand and drags her to the back and wraps both arms around her, holding her tight. Tears slide down her face and onto her friend's shoulder. "You should've told me sooner."

Cerita breaks the embrace, now softened and tearful. "I couldn't. It's nothing special for us. It's just us. There was nothing to tell, and Mom just lost her job yesterday."

"Remember how Mom said that my dad would be back by today?"

"Yeah."

"He's still not home. Mom still won't tell me about the task he was given, or why."

"Your dad's business trips have been known to run long before." Cerita runs a hand over her cheek.

"I've always known what those trips were about." Jenna looks down at her hands. "I haven't been a good friend and I'm sorry."

It's Cerita's turn to embrace her friend. "No.

You've been a good friend. I just keep life to myself."

"It's time we both change that. I'm going to talk to my mom about yours. She's in personnel and she'd know if there's something available." Jenna gives her another squeeze. "I can't help you come around to the reality of who you are, but I'll always be your friend."

"I'm sorry for yelling earlier. This is just so hard."

A slight lift in the corners of Jenna's mouth shows her friend something else. "Once you come to terms with all of that, you'll start learning a lot more that will throw you for a loop."

Cerita's eyes roll. "That is not what I want to hear."

The sound of the door opening gets both of their attention. Jenna notices the time on the clock over Cerita's shoulder. Her face brightens. "You need to wipe your face off in the bathroom. I'm pretty sure that's your company."

Cerita runs her hands over her tear stained face while she nearly runs to the employee restroom to clean up. By the time she makes it to the front again, James is sitting in the lobby with two plates of pizza on the back coffee table, and Jenna is lighting a candle between them. There is a carnation resting on the table behind one of the plates. Her face warms deeply, and her eyes threaten to tear again.

As she steps around the desk to join them,

she notices James' hair has been cut. The back is cropped short against his head and the front is longer, hanging forward from his ears to face. When he brushes his bangs back, his ears seem to disappear altogether. The moment his deep eyes meet hers, she swallows hard and smiles.

He stands and shifts his weight. "I um . . . hungry?"

She studies him carefully, noting the black jeans and vest over a white button down. Dress shoes replace his usual black and green sneakers. "This is a lot more than I was expecting." Her eyes turn to the table. "Thank you."

He runs a hand through his hair. "I can't take all the credit. But," he slides over to grab the flower and extends it to her, "this is for you."

Absently, Cerita tucks a piece of hair behind her ear, and takes the flower from his hand. "Thanks."

"Hate to interrupt you love birds, but lunch break is only forty minutes. I'll need her help getting the computers to work with me on the end of week stuff." Jenna grins and nearly skips back behind the desk.

James reaches for Cerita's hand and guides her to the couch in front of the table. "So . . ."

"So . . ." Her eyes drift to the pizza again. "Looks good."

He half smiles. "It's homemade."

"Really? I wouldn't have known by looking at it."

"You'll know when you taste it." He leans over, picks up a plate, and then extends it to her. His hand shakes a little. He puts his second hand around the other side of the plate to steady it. "I guess I'm nervous."

Her smile grows a bit. "So am I."

"I hope you like it."

She takes a nibble. The first bite is rich in flavor, and savory. The meat is cut into small slivers that melt in her mouth, and the cheese blends perfectly to compliment it. "Mmm . . ."

His face brightens, and he digs into his own slice. "I'm glad that you like it."

"It is wonderful. Who made this?"

"I did."

Her eyes widen. "I had no idea you could cook like this. What's the meat?"

His face drops a little. "Well, it's not a usual meat you'd put on a regular pizza."

She pauses her meal. "Okay?"

"It's lamb. It's cooked well, then the excess grease from it is dried out a bit before it's added to the cheese blend." He speaks with authority, but his face reddens.

"It's delicious." She finishes her piece, savoring every bite. "You're an expert with this."

"Yeah, well . . . yeah, kind of."

"We need to stop this nervousness . . . I think we're both stuck in it." Cerita attempts to sound assertive, but feels the butterflies crowding her pizza.

"How do you suggest we do that?"

"I don't know. I mean we've been in school together and in the same classes for a while. Shouldn't this be easier?"

He half nods. "Maybe. I don't know. I've never been on a date of any kind where I actually liked the girl first. Not before tonight."

She pinches her eyebrows together. "You take delicious meals to girls you don't like?"

He laughs. "No, not that. I . . . Mom and Dad have their ideas and make arrangements for me with friends and stuff. I go to appease them."

"Ah . . ." She smiles a bit larger as the word 'date' sinks in. "So, kinda, sorta both of our first kinda dates?"

"You've never been on a date? Not even homecoming?"

"That wasn't a date. That was . . . um, mom's friend's son not having someone to appear with." She shakes her head. "Never really had the time for anything like that."

"If Jenna hadn't told me to come by, you would have just avoided me then?" He shifts in the seat to face her better.

"Maybe?" She shrugs. "I've had a couple of people ask me out, but I'm just not into this usually. I work, get school stuff done, and help my mom out."

"I can understand that, and respect it. It's good to be there for your family." James pulls on the bottom of his shirt with one hand and leans back on his other arm. "You have a younger brother, right?"

"Actually two, and a younger sister. Carlos is twelve, Ciro is four, and Carolina is nearly three."

"That's a big family."

"Yes it is. How about you? Any brothers or sisters?"

James nods. "Yes. I have two older brothers and a younger sister. Both brothers own small farms outside of town and my sister stays home helping my mom out. She's not in school yet. Dad's often out west with the ranch too, so we stay busy most of the time."

"I never pegged you to be a farm boy."

He shrugs. "I know, I'm too cool for that." He almost winks.

She laughs and finally feels herself relaxing.

From the desk they hear, "Okay, Cerita. Enough flirting. Time to get work done."

James straightens up. "If it's okay, I'd like to stay to walk you to your car at the end of the shift."

"I'd like that." Cerita stands, and he stands with her. "Dinner was both beautiful and delicious. The company was the best part though."

He leans over and kisses her cheek. "I have to agree."

Her eyes drop and her smile broadens as she makes her way back to the desk.

"See, told you there was nothing to be

nervous about." Jenna stands at her usual terminal. "Now, help me get the weekly reports running and organized for tomorrow."

"Yeah." Cerita works alongside her friend while James cleans up the dinner area. For the next two hours, the girls move through each item on their task list more comfortable than before. Whenever it's possible, James is included in the conversation.

They deliver the customer reports for the longer stay guests and finish the nightly report scheduling for after close. As they collect their bags and finalize the night, both girls find themselves double checking all of the paperwork. Finally, they lock the door and move to the cars.

Jenna's phone rings. "It's Mom. I'll take this and you two say goodbye." She drops into the car to talk.

Cerita smiles without taking her gaze from James' eyes. "Thank you for making tonight nice."

"I'm glad I could. Jenna told me you've had a rough few days. If there's ever something I can do, I'm here."

"Thanks. Most of this is stuff I have to work out on my own."

He shrugs. "We all have that."

"Yeah . . ."

"So, can we do this again sometime? Maybe at a park, or restaurant or something that's not work?" James leans against her car.

"I'd like that."

"Good. I'm looking forward to it." He sighs. "I guess we should go."

"Jenna's mom usually has a conniption when she's a few minutes later than expected so . . . yeah, we should."

He opens her car door for her and waits until she is seated to close it. After leaning over and giving her another kiss on the cheek, he says, "I'll see you in school. When I do, you'll have to pinch me so I know it isn't a dream."

Her face warms.

James stands and slides into the car next to her. It's different than the one he takes to school. It's a two door instead of four. The soft, blue hues reflect in various shades off the street lights. She tries to etch it into her memory.

Jenna gets off the phone and nudges Cerita. "We've got to get going, but I have good news for your mom."

Her mind comes back into the moment. She starts the car and pulls out, with James behind her. "What's up?"

Jenna pulls out her bookbag and scribbles an address on the paper. "Have your mom be at this office tomorrow morning. It's my mom's. She's got an open position that will be a big help for her. It's got steady hours, salary instead of hourly, and benefits. I don't know what all of that will involve, but Mom's really certain that your mom would be a great fit."

"Nice. Tuck it into my bag please? I'll give it to her when I get home."

"Of course." Jenna turns and tucks the paper into the unused drink pouch on the side of her friend's backpack.

"What's the job?" Cerita turns down Jenna's road, and notices James go straight in her rear view mirror. A pang of disappointment strikes her unexpectedly.

"Not a clue." Jenna giggles. "Mom was very enthusiastic when I told her what your mom's been doing and how long and stuff. She got to talking about things and forgot to tell me the job. I didn't think to ask."

"Wow. Okay. This is good. And your mom makes the hiring choices?"

"I'm pretty sure that's the case."

"Sweet. I'm looking forward to bringing good news to my mom." Cerita parks in her friend's driveway as usual. "Thanks for everything tonight."

She shrugs. "I didn't do much. I just added the candle. He's got it bad for you."

"Yeah."

"And you've got it bad for him too."

"Yeah."

Jenna giggles. "You two do make a good couple, but just take your time being one, okay?"

"I'd have to have time to be a couple. If I find time to actually go out on a date with him, I'll be surprised."

"You could tomorrow. We don't work on Saturday."

"We didn't exchange numbers or anything and . . . no. I've got things to sort out." She pauses for a moment. "You'll tell me when your dad is home?"

Jenna nods. "I will."

"Thanks again."

"Right. Still no need to thank me, but I'll take it." Jenna hugs her friend quickly, grabs her bag and heads inside.

When Cerita makes it home, she shares the news with her mom, while watching her light up with hope easing her mind. The mother and daughter talk for a bit. Cerita tells her mom about the evening at work and the dinner with James. By midnight they both make their way to bed.

The next afternoon, the mood in the house starts to change.

Carmen enters the house after her visit with Jenna's mother. Her face is relaxed and she calls her children to her in the living room. "I have good news. Jenna's mom, Mrs. Williams, introduced me to my weekend team today. Starting Monday, I will be the new executive sanitation manager with Thenbold Manufacturing and Properties. We visited the main sites today. On Monday we'll visit all of the sites I will be overseeing. My hours end at three, so Carlos, you won't have to babysit after school every day. I'll still be on call, so there may be times when I'll have to leave suddenly."

"Mom, that's great!" Carlos settles on the couch next to her and his eyes fall on his older sister who is leaning in the doorway by the kitchen. "See, I knew things would work out."

Cerita can't help but smile.

Carolina curls onto her mom's lap.

Her mom continues, "I will only work the weekends I want to, and we have salary coming in now instead of hourly. Benefits that will cover every one of us begin in six months if everything works out." Mom's enthusiasm is contagious. Ciro starts wandering around the house cheering 'Mommy!' while Carolina snuggles close. Carlos watches with a large grin on his face.

"I know this is going to be great, Mom."

She turns her head to Cerita. "If you want to quit your job, in one month, we will be fine without it."

The thought had never occurred to her, so Cerita shrugs. "Maybe we can think it over?"

"Of course, dear. Thank you for making the contact for me." Carmen tucks Carolina under her arm and carries her across the room. Embracing her older daughter, she kisses the girl on the cheek. "I'm proud of you, mi hija."

"Thanks, Mom."

Chapter 3

Ralph stands just off of the mats. His arms are folded across his chest as he watches two of his students spar. He finds each of their movements flow with ease, and each capitalizes on their strengths. The shift from one side of the mat to the other makes no difference to either one of them. This impresses upon him that these students are working hard and preparing for the next level of training.

Without a word, he steps onto the mat, grabs the arm of the young man and pulls him to the ground while the young woman spins a kick at his chest. He blocks her kick by grabbing her ankle and pulling her off balance. Both students lie on the ground breathless. "Good job."

Both bound to their feet again and bow to him, then to each other out of respect.

"Serena, you need to watch your extension. Had the kick landed, you were still far enough away that the impact would have been nominal. Step into the kick next time."

"Yes, Master Fredrickson." The dark complected girl bows as she speaks. Her hair remains pulled tight and her eyes shimmer with delight in her exhaustion.

The master then turns to the boy. "Your punches are good. They land hard and solid, but you are holding back from someone who can handle them. Don't. You won't master the skills effectively. I wouldn't partner you with Serena if she couldn't handle it. You won't know when you're using too much power behind something if you don't give it your all."

The dark haired boy bows. "Yes, Master Fredrickson."

"Good job both of you. I will see you next week." Ralph watches his students for a moment before they disappear into their respective changing areas. His mind wanders to his uncommitted apprentice, wondering what it will take to get her to the same level as the two in the room, or better.

A flash of light from the corner of the room alerts him of a waiting message. He activates the projection to find a tall, long haired woman standing opposite him. Her serious nature concerns him. "Hello, Vivian. You have a message from the council I assume?"

"Knight Fredrickson, I do." The slightest hint of her ear tips peek out from the hair draping over her shoulders. "The council would like to greet your chosen apprentice by the Choosing."

"The council has a problem then. She hasn't accepted. She just had her world turned upside down, why would they expect she'd jump into training within days?" His brow knits. "You are expecting far too much of her."

"They are expecting her to accept her place. They are expecting you to assist her in doing so."

"My job is to train her and prepare her to take over for me when the time comes. It is not to convince her that everything she knows is the fantasy. That's the job of a homo-supreme's parents, and she doesn't have one available." His voice is terse and he rubs his thumb into the palm of the opposite hand. "There is little for me to work with, and more expectations."

Vivian's voice remains unchanged and devoid of emotion. "Your task has been given. In one month's time, you will deliver her to Atlantis for the Choosing."

"And if she refuses her position?"

"Then your position will be adjusted as well." Vivian waves her hand and her projection disappears.

Ralph grumbles under his breath.

His male student approaches him from

behind. "I thought I heard Aunt Vivian's voice."

"You did, James. She's not on my good side right now."

"She has a way of doing that." He ties a headband over the tips of his ears. "I can talk to her if you want me to. I doubt it would matter. In her mind, if you're not at least fifty, you're far too young to have any sense."

"It's fine. I just have to get my apprentice to begin her training. Not an easy task when you consider they have selected her and she's not chosen to step up yet. I don't know what's so special about this girl, but she's being actively sought by the council."

"This is the girl you were mentioning to me before?"

"Yes. I think she's in your school. Although, if I'm going to be able to bring her to your level fast enough for the Choosing in a month, I may have to find a way to convince her."

"I thought knights had to serve willingly."

"They do. That's what has me confused." Ralph crosses the room with James striding next to him. "I have never known the council to enforce a specific apprentice before, nor to attempt to do so while they were yet unaware of the full extent of who they are."

"I came to train to become the Knight's Guide, but I came to train with a knight in training, as is custom. If an apprentice isn't found, I'm supposed to go to Atlantis for the

Choosing myself and be selected by another. Can I help you bring the apprentice into her position?" James squares himself to the Knight.

"I'll give it some thought."

"If I am not being rude, Master Knight, might I ask her name?"

"Cerita Guzman. She's about your homo-sapien age."

James drops his eyes to the mat. "She's in a lot of my classes and I had no idea."

Ralph lifts an eyebrow. "Is there something you should tell me?"

"We've been on a date. Last night. It was . . ." A slight grin perks his cheek. ". . . really nice."

"I see. You didn't mimic typical human behaviors at this stage did you?"

"I am an elf. I have my standards, and the claiming should be understood before such actions are taken."

"Good. I would hate to share with your Aunt Vivian that you've defiled your position and clan with your actions."

James looks at the knight through narrowed eyes and a clenched jaw. "Never."

"Good, good." The older man sighs. "You are faced with another problem now. You are emotionally involved with your knight in a way that may not be conducive to either of your missions."

"I will not permit such interference."

"James, there is a galactic consequence if you

do. Mind your position, and hers." Ralph settles in a chair behind the wooden desk. "Next Saturday, if you can bring her in, that would be helpful." His eyes rest on the computer monitor in front of him. "I am sure we have some things available here to help her come to terms with several facts, and perhaps accept her position."

"I can do this for you, Master Knight."

"Thank you." Ralph looks up at the young elf. "You are invaluable in everything. I trust you will make the right choices along the way."

"Thank you. Coming from you, that means a great deal."

"You should get home. I'm sure your mother has many tasks ahead of you."

James nods with a hint of a smile. "I'm sure she does too. New chickens were sent in from the ranch earlier and Dad's promised to be home for dinner. There's a lot to do to prepare."

"With your father, I'm sure of that." Ralph allows his cheeks to lift. "Give them both my regards."

"Of course, Master Knight." James strolls out of the training facility and to his car.

The week at school goes by. He sees Cerita every chance he can during the day, but attempts to keep a distance. Knowing what he knows makes the whole notion of becoming involved with her very different. His responsibility is greater than the longings of his heart, and he reminds himself of this daily. On Thursday after school, he meets her at her car.

"Did you mean it when you said we could do something together outside of here?" He smiles.

Her big brown eyes meet his. She nibbles on her lower lip and nods. "Yes."

"Good. Have you ever done martial arts before?"

She shakes her head. "No. I can't say I have, but I'm interested in it."

He grins. "Well, I take a class every Saturday, usually, sometimes more. Anyway, I thought I'd invite you to come with me. It's usually just me and the teacher. It's pretty advanced, but your company would be great."

"I don't know. I'd be a beginner." She shifts on her feet.

"It would be a lot of fun, and some good exercise. Come just once and if you hate it, no big. I'm sure we'll find something else fun." He tilts her chin up slightly. "Please join me this weekend?"

"Okay." She moves to kiss him, but he meets her cheek instead.

"I'll pick you up about ten in the morning. Or I will, if you can trust me with your address."

"Do I have reason not to trust you?"

He chuckles. "I would hope not."

She pulls out paper and a pencil and scribbles her address and phone number for him. "So, see you tomorrow?"

"And Saturday." He smiles and makes his way back to his car. His pulse is racing and his face feels hot.

When he pulls in at home, his mother greets him. "How was school?"

He shrugs. "Okay, I guess." He starts down the path to his loft over the barn with his mom. "You remember that girl I told you about?"

"The one with the eyes that make you weak in the knees?"

He chuckles. "Yeah, that one."

"What about her?" She wipes her hands off on the apron she's wearing as they walk.

"Master Knight asked me to bring her in, and she agreed to visit his training center on Saturday."

"Then you've done well. You should be proud." She smiles. "Planning to tell her about your family? Or traditions? This fast?"

"It's only partly like that, Mom. Really, after speaking to the master last weekend, I'm not sure about all of that yet. Seems the council has picked her as apprentice."

"And you believe that the way you feel about this girl would complicate your service?" She stops her son, and spins him to look at her.

"Yes. I didn't know before the pizza on Friday, or . . ." He sighs. "I just want to protect our kind from what may come."

"I know, James. I know. Spirited, focused, and

loving. It's a hard balance to achieve, but you've always made good choices. Your heart shouldn't be ignored though. Balance the two, and you'll find what you need when you need it." She leans up and kisses her son's cheek. "You're a wise boy."

"Thanks, Mom. I've got a bit of homework, and then more training for tonight. Do you need anything done around here?" He gestures toward the field outside the barn.

"Nope. Your usual supply for the animals each night will be enough." She looks over to see her youngest running toward her. "Dinner is already cooking. Come in once your homework is complete and I'll have a heaping plate for you."

"I will." He slings the bookbag over his shoulder again, and scales the ladder to his loft.

** *** **

"Hey . . ." James frowns. He knows what needs to be done, but doing it frustrates him. "You ready to go?"

"Almost. I want to grab something." Cerita runs back to her room, lifts the corner of her mattress, and pulls out the dagger she was gifted. Something in her gut tells her she'll need it.

In a few minutes, she is riding along in James' car on the way to some martial arts class she has never heard of before. The idea of learning a new skill entertains her and spending time with James makes the thought of the class worth it. It only takes a few moments in silence before they arrive at the building.

He is out of the car first. He rounds the vehicle quickly and opens the door for her. "You're going to really like my teaching master. He's fantastic and really helps you out along the way. He makes extra time if you need it or set a goal or something." He walks her to the door and opens it, waiting for her to enter before him.

"Sounds promising." Cerita steps lightly through the door.

James follows closely behind. "I've got to change. You can wait here. The master teacher will be out in a moment."

She stands in the center of the mats. The wall to her right is mirrored. The wall to her left has three doors, one is marked male, another is marked weapons, and the last is marked female. She reasons the two gender identified are locker rooms. The other seems to be another training room. Ahead are two additional unmarked doors. Before her curiosity gets the best of her, she hears footsteps. Turning toward them makes her stomach jump.

"Welcome, Cerita." The old man she knows to be the knight stands before her.

"Hi." She takes a deep breath. "You're the teacher?"

"I am." He steps onto the mat facing her.

"Are you ready to become my apprentice?"

"You don't give a girl time to think do you?" Cerita presses her lips into a thin line.

"Your mom has a nice new job, doesn't she?"

Her eyes grow wide. "You aren't threatening her are you? She's happy for the first time in as long as I can remember. So, help me -"

He puts a hand up stopping her. "It's nothing like that, Cerita. She's not going to lose the job if you don't take your positions as apprentice."

She grumbles out loud, "Good."

"Something happened the first night we met that I've not seen happen before. You, a young woman among the homo-sapiens, activated my sword. This was only unusual because homo-sapiens should not be capable of this. It appears you're not only capable, but sought after. Although I do need an apprentice, I was seeking one that would be far younger. They are more easily trained and adaptable. I'm not really certain you're up for such a rigorous task."

"What? You want to teach me to fight and you think I'm too slow to pick up on it?" She folds her arms over her chest. "You don't know a thing about me."

"I know more than you realize. Obviously the job your mom has should have tipped you off to that fact. Now, give me one reason I should teach you to take my place."

"No." She's indignant in her tone. "Your council made that call, not me. I don't want this. I don't want anything to do with this." When her eyes catch a glimpse of James emerging in his fighting gear, she scowls. "You knew about this. You two teamed up to corner me. You tricked me!"

James feels sweat bead at his hairline. He runs a hand over the back of his neck. "No. I mean kinda, but . . . Cerita, *please*. The knight's apprentice is important. You're important."

"I know nothing about this stuff. I don't want to. I have a life. I have a family that needs me. Why do you think I should want anything to do with this?"

Ralph nods to his student and in the blink of an eye, the young man stands near the exit. "You brought your dagger today. You were not aware you'd be here, but something urged you to bring it."

"I just hoped the teacher could show me something with it. Ya never know what kinds of freaks you'll run 'cross the fields at night." Her jaw is tense, squared. Her eyes narrow to near slits.

"That was it?" The master knight does not allow her quip to reflect in his tone or stance.

"Yes."

"Okay then. Go. Enjoy your ignorance of the reality around you."

She spins on heel and squares with James. "Take me home."

His eyes drop and his face slackens before he

nods. "I'll be another moment to change, and I'll take you home."

He's gone before she can blink.

Ralph remains in the center of the room. He considers his words carefully before speaking again. "How old are you, Cerita?"

"I thought you knew everything about me." Her tone is biting, and she keeps her back is to him.

"At your age, you can make choices that affect more than just your small sphere. You are on the ledge of one of those choices, and you are walking away from the part you're intended to play. The limited I know, this is a habit that's in your blood."

She squares with him and starts to stalk closer. "What are you implying?"

"I'm implying nothing. I'm stating clearly that you are not the first of your family to avoid an important responsibility."

James emerges again. His headband is in his pocket and he tucks one lock of hair that falls in his face behind his pointed ear. "You ready?"

Through gritted teeth, she responds, "Yes."

He holds the door for her, and she steps outside with James on her heels. He opens the car door and she says nothing to him. Once they are driving again, he finds himself increasingly uncomfortable with the intensity of her anger. As they approach the edge of town to turn toward her road, he chooses to pass it. Instead, he continues driving.

She snaps at him. "What are you doing?"

"I want to show you something." James drives out into the country and down the roads toward his home. "First, I need to grab some things."

When he gets out of the car, he greets his mother and explains himself while Cerita remains in the car. He moves swiftly upstairs to his loft. Grabbing his sword and changing into his boots, he knows he's taking a big risk that needs preparation. He grabs a small, leaf styled band and secures it to his neck. "By the creations, I hope I don't need this."

As he drops down from the ledge to the ground, he braces himself for the heat of her anger again. He slides into the car and pulls out again, heading down the first dirt road into the countryside.

"What's the garb?"

"I'm a knight's guide in training. Master Knight Fredrickson had one when he began too, but that . . . he lost his life defending the knight early in their careers and no one else worked out." James keeps his eyes on the road to avoid her glare.

"Where are you taking me?" Her voice remains tense.

"To a meeting." He drives straight ahead, trying to concentrate on the roads and his destination. He attempts to avoid glancing at her, with her body still so obviously stiff in the seat next to him. "Once it's over, I'll take you home, nothing further." He sighs. "I won't contact you, even in school, if you'd prefer it."

She looks out the window as they drive, silently fuming.

The roads change. They shift from pavement to gravel, and eventually to dust. Houses become fields, and fields seem to stretch into forests and rivers. When the car finally comes to a stop, her stomach tells her it's well past lunch time.

James turns in the car, grabs a bag out of the back seat and tosses her an apple. "Eat up. You'll need your strength. We still have some walking to do."

Without a word, she crunches into the apple.

He climbs out and opens the trunk of the car, pulling out a wooden device and a bag full of assorted items. Slinging the bag over his shoulder leads him to recall that his wristband additions are tucked under the carpet. He withdraws two shiny stems and attaches them one at a time to each wristband. As he moves to her door, the wrist bands become cuffs, which then extend up to his elbow. The sun reflects off the silver metal as the door is pulled open. "Sorry. It can be bright out here."

She shields her eyes as she steps out. "What are those?"

"It's the rest of my gear. We're meeting a small wer-pack to tell them that there are some human hunters coming."

"Human hunters?"

"Yes. There have always been groups of hunters who seek to eliminate our kind. Some get to know the groups they think are immortal in their patrol areas. Most are less patient and seek to kill all other hominids. Knights were put in place by the council when the first hunters nearly eliminated a wolfpack centuries ago." He adjusts his bag, slides the wooden device into his hip holder, and secures the remainder of his gear. "You have that dagger?"

She slides it out of her pocket. "Yes."

"Good. Don't lose it. Stay close so you don't get lost. A warm meal will be waiting when we get to the den."

He starts into the trees at a firm pace that she struggles to maintain. They trek along a path not easily identified. They move through the forest long enough to lose track of time. Silence hangs between them through the longest part of their walk. He pauses his step when a new set of footfalls joins the chorus of their feet. James listens carefully to the way the steps fall, until a large, brown wolf finally comes near them. The wolf sniffs the elf, and then the girl before rolling on his back for a rub.

"Good boy, Brownie." James kneels and pets the animal.

Cerita stands back, watching and wondering when this animal will become a hominid.

"You don't have to be shy. He doesn't bite those who are here with his den. Brownie and I have been good friends for a while now." James looks down at the animal. "Haven't we, boy?"

The wolf makes a sound similar to a soft bark.

Hesitantly, she steps forward. "He's not . . . ahh werwolf?"

James chuckles. "Brownie? No, not at all. He's just a wolf, and a self-fashioned protector of the den. Not everything you meet in the woods is human."

He stands and gestures forward. The wolf takes off running. "Not sure how he got here. His breed isn't common to this area, but he's attached himself to the Von der Slin family and their den mates. We're not far now. Just about another half a mile."

"That's not far to you? My feet hurt. My legs are sore and burning, and my arms are stiff. Another half a mile might as well be twelve." Her tone is terse, her brow is knit, and she is fighting the urge to cry out in frustration.

"You should exercise more." He moves to follow the wolf at a much slower pace.

She grunts and reluctantly follows him.

After what feels as long as it took them to approach the den, they finally reach a clearing with several log cabins in them. A large two story cabin sits in the center of the clearing. It has an active chimney that billows out a sweet, smoky aroma which urges her stomach forward. They approach the large home and climb the two stairs onto the porch. He knocks firmly and a petite woman comes to the door.

She has long black hair and soft blue eyes. The woman eyes Cerita closely, smiling only when her gaze meets James'. "Hello, dear elf. Have you come to speak with my parents?"

He nods. "If they are around."

"Mother is cooking a meal, as are the other mothers." She opens the door wider and gestures for him to enter. "Please, step inside."

"Thank you, Cercy. This is a friend. Her name is Cerita." He gestures toward the dark haired woman. "This is Cercy, she's the Alpha family's eldest daughter."

Cerita extends her hand. "It's good to meet you."

Cercy lifts her eyebrows and accepts the grasp of the girl, while sliding slightly closer to James. "It is good to make friends with a friend of our dear James here. He's been such a help for the pack, I can't begin to express enough gratitude."

Cerita's eyes tighten ever so slightly. "I'm sure you'll do your best though." She withdraws her hand. "May we sit down?"

"Of course. I'll get my parents." She steps from the room with a sway in her hips, glancing over her shoulder just enough to see the pair as she exits.

Cerita's eyes trace the high ceiling. Hanging from the center is a large chandelier. While the large, ornate chandelier is brightly-lit through a decorative glass, the outer ring has traditionally lit candles. Framing it on the floor above is a large winding staircase that extends to the first floor in a grand fashion. The center of the open room is a large fireplace that separates one section of the room from another. The couch they rest on is made of wood, with cushions that are deep, thick, and far more comfortable than she was prepared for. Before Cerita is able to fully relax, Cercy returns with two others, both of whom are slightly taller than she is.

James stands, urging Cerita to do the same. With great effort, she brings herself to her feet again.

"Hello, Mr. Von der Slin, Mrs. Von der Slin. This is my associate, Cerita. She's going witness our discussion."

Mrs. Von der Slin slides around James and embraces Cerita. "It is a pleasure to have you here, dear." She turns her head toward her daughter. "Cercy, have you brought our guests beverages yet?"

"Not yet. I'll do so now." Cercy's eyes linger on the elf for several moments before she exits again to attend to her mother's request.

Mrs. Von der Slin returns her focus to the human. "My daughter often forgets her manners in the presence of a pretty face. I'm sure you know what that is like." She smiles broadly and settles the girl onto the couch again. "You look quite worn out. I'll see to it you get a great meal and some room to stretch."

Mr. Von der Slin gestures to the other couch, while settling himself in a large chair that rests between the two. "You bring us news?"

"Yes, sir, I do." James leans forward on his knees. "The hunters have agreed to respect your hunting grounds as long as you limit them to the area immediately around your clearing. Their leader, Edward Jones, is a reasonable man. He is willing to meet you personally and discuss any details and concerns they have. His second lieutenant is a bit more brash, quick to flare in temper, and faster to aggression. Thankfully, Mr. Jones has kept him in his place."

Mr. Von der Slin's dark hair hangs over his face when he leans toward James. "Can we consider this Jones fellow an ally?"

"I believe he is, at least, not an enemy. He prefers peace between the various hominid species, and wants details on who is where and how many."

"I suppose he is expecting you to provide this information?" the gentle motherly voice of Mrs. Von der Slin chimes in.

"Actually, they have yet to meet a knight and have requested the Master Knight to provide such information personally. I have advised him of the situation."

"And he has agreed to this?" the older woman inquires again.

"He has agreed to disclose only the information about those who are segregated by choice within the county." James turns toward Mr. Von der Slin. "Sir, that means only a small handful of areas will be patrolled, it will include your hunting grounds from time to time. I believe if you make yourself welcoming of the hunters on patrol, there will be limited concerns."

"Well, we see no reason to do anything else." He places the tips of his large, hairy hands together. "We do not choose to live separate from the other hominids to avoid them, merely to live as we desire in safety and peace."

Suddenly, a soft howl is heard from the floor above. Cerita jerks her head toward the stairs and two energetic balls of fur come bounding down the stairs. After a quick jaunt around the room, Mrs. Von der Slin corrals them and pulls them into her arms. "Victor, Vincent, this is our guest, Cerita. She's joining us for today. Best manners, okay?"

One of the boys smiles at her. His face is distinctly human, and his hands are larger than one would expect for a human child. From the top of his head straight down his back is excessively long hair. "Hi, Miss Cerita."

The other boy crawls up onto the couch, lays his head on her lap, and closes his eyes. "You're warm." He yawns.

She smiles warmly and places her hand on his shoulder. "I'm glad that you're comfortable."

The boy rolls over so his face is looking up at her. "You're pretty."

She laughs. "You're cute too." Leaning over, she places a soft kiss on his furry forehead.

"My twins. My last litter, I hope." Mrs. Von der Slin smiles. "Boys are such a handful and so full of energy. I don't think these two would know what to do if they were ever separated. It's a pleasure to see them taking to you so quickly too."

Cercy returns with a tray of drinks. She places it on the coffee table. "Please help yourself. It's southern sweet tea. Enough for all to enjoy." She smiles sweetly as she lifts a glass toward James. "I made certain to limit the ice in yours, as you prefer."

His eyes dart briefly to Cerita before accepting the tea. "Thank you."

Cercy takes another glass and settles herself next to him.

Mr. Von der Slin clears his throat. Once he has the attention of the room again, he asks, "When is the meeting expected?"

"Later this evening. About dinner time, maybe." James remains on the edge of the couch. "The master knight will contact me once he meets with Mr. Jones. I should also get notice that the meeting is starting, but I doubt it will be more than an acknowledgment. I will remain here until we know the results, to assure you are aware of them as it occurs."

Cerita's eyes grow wide. Although her muscles ache and her body has become comfortable in the cushy couch, she was not expecting to be out all day. She isn't prepared to remain as a guest in this odd environment. She makes a mental note to rip into James, again, the first moment she's able to express herself.

"If you would approve, Mr. Von der Slin, it would be good if we could do a brief security walk." His hand gestures toward Cerita. "Making her aware of the general domain while assuring the safety of the families would be beneficial."

"Absolutely. Am I or my wife required for this?"

"No, sir. Not this time. Should I see anything of concern, I will make you aware of it." James stands, places the glass on the tray again and gestures for Cerita to join him.

She tickles the little guy on her lap, and he curls into a giggling ball. "You be good for your folks, and we'll play a bit when I'm back."

"Okay." He smiles broadly, showing some of his sharper teeth as he does.

With effort, she stands and follows James out of the house to the edges of the tree line. He walks while remaining attentive to everything around them. "If you see another being that you don't expect to, tell me."

"What should I be expecting? You dragged me out to the middle of nowhere without any clue what's up. You tell me we'll be here all day, only after I'm so drained and in pain that I can't function well. Now you've got me looking for something I don't expect to see? I didn't expect to see people who look half like wolves but that's all the kids out here." Her brow knits. Her jaw sets.

His hand gestures to a handful of children a bit older than the twins in the home of the Von der Slins. "They haven't been fit with their microbots yet. The bots control their instincts, appearance, and allow them to fit into sapien society. That's why you don't see it in their parents, or any other adults."

"And without the bots, they become wolves?"

His eyes scrunch when he laughs. "You watch entirely too much television and movies. They are hominids, just not like the sapiens we go to school with. The wers have the extra hairline, or fur, as you see on the children. They tend to be much stronger than sapiens and really than most hominids. They are certainly faster too. Each type of wer has their own traditions, some have their own clans, or dens if you will." He gestures to the now busy area around the small cluster of homes. "We have some that reject the old ways and live among the sapiens for different reasons. Often, their children are fitted with microbots at birth, and those will need modifications over time, thus they visit the city many times in life."

They continue to walk while they talk. Over time, Cerita's strides continue to get longer and the stiffness seems to subside. "Okay, so wers don't become animals, they just resemble them and a human?"

"They *are* human, Cerita." He gestures to a cluster of boys and girls in the center of the houses. "They play like all children. They have parents who love them, teach them, support them, and help them make their own choices."

She slows her steps, watching the wer-children run and laugh like her siblings do. Other than the physical differences, she can't identify things that make them unique from the world she knows. Instead of being focused on the tree line she watches the adults walk from one home to another carrying large pots or other items. When hanging clothing outside, many of the different families chat about their day, and workload, like everyone she knows. When one woman trips moving up stairs to her porch, three of her neighbors stop what they are doing to check on her, and help her collect what drops.

Her attention is drawn to several men entering the far end of the circle. They carry large beasts draped over their shoulders. They are clearly respected as hunters when they are greeted by everyone they encounter. When one hunter tells another man that he'll save a leg for his family, Cerita can't help but smile. This small community is inter-reliant in all the best ways possible.

James continues to walk around the edge of the tree line. Upon finding everything as it should be, his attention is drawn to the would-be-knight beside him. Noticing her attention focused on the den's hunters, he mentions, "There are several families in this pack."

"They all seem to work together."

"They do. Most find a way to co-exist with each other and nature." He gestures to the area where the hunters laid the large deer. "Someone will help them clean the animals. They'll leave some food for their wolf friends. The rest will be either pared out to the families or frozen for later. Nothing will go to waste. Even bones are ground up for compost for their crops."

Cerita turns her eyes toward him. "Crops?"

"This pack keeps indoor greenhouses."

Her attention returns to the pack activities as they walk the perimeter. "There are so few differences and this feels peaceful here."

"Normally it's very peaceful here. Actually, the only time I've not encountered peace here was when a lone hunter stumbled into the den. The alpha, Mr. Von der Slin, had to determine his motives and what to do with him. Several suggested . . . well, some of the pack didn't want him to leave." James clears his throat.

"But he did?"

"Yes, he did. He was honestly lost. The alpha recognized this, provided him with water, and sent him home." He hears one of the wolves growl. His eyes dart to find a small bear wandering toward the tree line. "Oh . . . they may be eating bear later this week too."

Cerita's brow furrows until she sees why. Finding a bear cub toddling toward the tree line where the pack homes are, she watches a few of the wolves attempt to scare the cub away. Ultimately, the cub wanders up a tree, and the wolves remain diligently on the edge of the den clearing, waiting and watchful. "I thought for sure they were going to hunt that cub down."

"Most wolves paired with a wer-pack don't need to. The pack hunts. The wolves have been known to help the pack, but they're more often protectors, and the first line of defense, by their own choice."

"So they won't attack the bear cub, unless the cub attacks?"

"Right. It's more likely the cub will stay in the tree until its mama bear comes, or until it can climb down on its own. Should the mother bear make it into the den, that's going to leave a whole new problem. It's likely, in that case, the hunters will assess the situation and make a choice for the safety of the pack."

"They don't always kill the bears?"

"Nah . . . if a mother is protecting their young, it's not uncommon for them to just knock the bear and her cubs unconscious and take them to a nearby cave to sleep the drugs off."

"Such a simple, peaceful existence. We don't see anything like this in our everyday."

"No. We see the results of competition and at

times, chaos, but there are other benefits." He gestures ahead of them. "We're nearly done with the patrol. While you didn't see much of the edge of the den, I think you saw something more important."

"People."

A soft smile lifts the corners of his lips. "There are many more on this world, and now others."

"I see there's a lot to learn here." She sighs. "I suppose it's time for a late lunch?"

"Yes. I'm sure it'll be ready when we get back."

Her soft brown eyes dart up toward his. "I'm sure Cercy will have your seat comfortably prepared and waiting for you."

He responds with a groan. "I'm sure." He sighs. "She was one of those arranged things I mentioned before. She doesn't get the 'not interested' part of things."

As his feet reach the porch, the door swings open. Cercy greets her returning guests. "The meal is ready and has just been placed on the table. Please, join us."

James encourages Cerita to enter first, and he follows behind with Cercy close to him. The hostess leads the pair into the dining room.

The dining room is brightly-lit by the broad windows on either side of the long table. Each chair is spaced with generous room. At one end are two chairs with cushions on them, giving the occupants the height needed to reach the table. From those chairs, two pair of eyes watch their guests with keen attention.

The head of the table has a chair with a taller back, and large arm rests. Around the table from there are chairs unified by design. All with high, wooden backs and soft seats.

A large, cooked bird is in the middle near the head of the table in front of Mr. Von der Slin. A pitcher of iced tea rests next to his plate, in front of where he is seating his wife as they enter. Behind the large bird are two types of vegetables, separated by a plate of warm, fragrant dinner rolls. Resting directly behind the turkey is a small plate of red fruit filled gelatin.

"You made it back. That's wonderful." Once his wife is settled comfortably, he sits in his chair. Extending his arms toward the table, he says, "Please, join us. The meal is hot. My wife and daughter make some of the best turkey anywhere."

Cercy guides James around the table, and waits until he pulls her chair out. As she settles, her eyes fall on Cerita who is moving a chair out on her own.

James settles into the open chair next to Cercy, across from Cerita.

One of the little boys jumps off his chair, runs to Cerita, and grabs both sides to pull it out for her. It's far enough and sudden enough that Cerita misses it while sitting down. She lands on the floor with a surprised noise. The boy urgently moves to help her up. "I'm so sorry. I'm so sorry."

James is on his feet. "Are you alright?"

Mrs. Von der Slin places her hand over her mouth. "Cerita, dear, are you alright?"

She smiles through her embarrassment. While standing, she allows the young boy to believe he's helped her up. "Thank you, Vincent."

"I'm Victor." He smiles with wet cheeks. "I wanted to hold your chair, like Daddy holds the chair for Mommy."

Cerita leans over and kisses the top of his head. "Thank you for your help, Victor."

His smile broadens, and he moves behind the chair again. They move it toward the table together and she finally settles.

James returns to the chair he was guided to.

Cercy's amusement is evident in her tone. "It is good he was so helpful."

Cerita looks over to Victor again with warmth. "Indeed. His help is always appreciated."

The boy beams as he crawls back into his chair again.

Mr. Von der Slin begins to carve the turkey and places it on a small platter that is then passed around the table. His wife takes the first slice and prepares plates for her youngest cubs. Once she's finished making their plates, she passes the vegetable dishes around the table, with the turkey plate following close behind.

Cerita picks up her fork before she realizes

she is the only one to do so. Cerita stops herself. She remains silent and attentive, watching for cues from the others at the table.

Mr. Von der Slin clears his throat as he settles behind his plate. He takes two bites. "This is delicious, my love." He leans over to kiss his wife before the rest of the table begins to enjoy the meal.

Cerita chides herself while taking the first few bites. When James fills her glass with tea, she addresses Mrs. Von der Slin, "Thank you for the delicious meal, and for welcoming me today." Her eyes turn to James briefly as he places her glass on the table. "Thank you."

"You are welcome, dear. Any of our cousins are welcome here." The elder woman's eyes light up as she responds.

Although the meal is delicious, and her hosts warm and welcoming, Cerita struggles with a nagging feeling that something isn't right. Working to dismiss it, she savors every bite but remains quiet while everyone around her engages in idle discussions.

Listening, she learns of the customs and plans for the day. She hears about hopes the sapien hunters will remain in peace among them. Her silence also allows her to hear how they came in contact with this group of hunters in the first place. She is impressed to learn that the alpha released an injured man who was brought to the village after spouting vile things at the werwolves carrying his injured body.

Cerita listens as the alpha explains the extent of the man's injuries, and what steps were needed to treat his wounds. It's made clear through his discussion that Mr. Von der Slin would prefer to heal his enemy than slay him, as the hunter had expected. By the end of the meal, she finds her mind drifting toward the meeting to come, and hoping for a positive outcome.

Once the table is cleared, Vincent and Victor approach Cerita. Victor asks, "Will you play with us?"

She nods. "I think I can do that. I'm sure James will tell me if he needs me."

"Of course I will." He watches as the twins drag Cerita outside.

For several moments, his gaze lingers long after she's gone. His mind whirls with the possible outcomes from the day spent among a new culture. Her acceptance of the cubs brings him hope for another opportunity to bring her into training. He is drawn from his thoughts when Cercy places her arm around his. He looks down at her arm, but remains silent and still.

"You like her?"

"My relationship with her is not of your concern, Cercy." He turns, pulling his arm from her grasp, and walks through the large house toward the backdoor.

Cercy easily keeps pace with him. "It is good

to know who my future partner will seek."

He sighs. "I have agreed to nothing. Our cultures are far too different to co-exist. We've been through that."

She shrugs. "So you keep telling me." She swings open the door to the greenhouse. "You'll find the quiet you're looking for in here."

"I'm aware." He moves over the threshold into a large room covered with a glass roof. Around each side are various plants in stages of development. In the center is a small waterfall with a bench around each of the four sides.

"You know, James, we have great things ahead of us. A strong alpha pair can lead two cultures and families together." She settles next to him on one of the benches. "We can begin to teach so many that our own planet isn't so lost that we need the outer planets."

He shakes his head. "You know the offworld developments are there for a reason. We may want the sapiens, and others, to accept such changes, but we can't force them to."

"Is that not a matter of perspective? Has Slyvia and Elrin not led the Cats and Wolves toward a mutual pack?"

"Cercy, that is a unique situation that remains localized on the wercat planet, in an isolated area. You've spoken of . . ." He closes his mouth, his eyes, and rests his hands on his legs before telling her, "I want to meditate."

"Of course." She leans against the back of the

bench.

"It is something to do alone."

"You really want me to leave, James?" Cercy leans toward him and wraps a finger in the longer length of his hair.

"Yes."

The wolf princess feigns hurt before rising. "As you desire, my alpha in the making."

He doesn't open his eyes. Instead, he listens in silence until she exits. Once she is gone, it takes him a little time to reach the ideal state of mind for meditation. His body relaxes. His mind evens and empties fully. The moment of peace stretches into hours. Hearing the sound of his communication device pulls him back to the moment. He glances at his wrist and finds the meeting has begun.

Minutes later, he meets the Von der Slins in the living room. After making them aware of the beginning of the meeting, the family settles down, minus only the twins, to enjoy some warm pie together. A loud noise erupts from the front door as two boundless balls of energy burst through dragging a weary human girl. They pull her into the living room, two furry hands on each of hers.

Victor proudly announces, "See, I told you Mom made pie."

Vincent adds, "And we always have it at dusk so we have full bellies for bedtime."

She laughs. "So I see." She then kneels down.

"Can you show me the washroom so I can get some of the dirt from our wrestling match off my hands and arms?"

Mrs. Von der Slin's long dark hair shifts as laughter rumbles through her body. "They had you rolling in the dirt, dear?"

"Oh, yes. And we climbed trees, ran races, and found out there's a secret base inside one of the large old trees not far from here." Cerita can't help but smile as she recalls her afternoon with the boys. They grab her hands and pull her from the room again. "I'll be back."

Their mother turns to their father. "Well, when we need time to ourselves, I know who to reach."

He chuckles. "They have taken quite a liking to her haven't they?"

"Yes, they most certainly have. It's great to see too, considering how few visitors we actually get here." She plunges her fork into the crust of her pie. "Cercy darling, I believe you've outdone yourself tonight."

The girl gestures with her head. "Thank you, Mother."

James finally allows himself to rest against the back of the couch with his plate. When the cubs drag a much cleaner Cerita into the room again, he watches them fight over who gets to sit next to her, and finds himself amazed by the gentleness with which she handles the debate. His mind drifts to the Knight's Guide pledge that looms ahead, and a sense of disappointment tugs at his heart.

Cerita barely gets two bites of her pie before a loud popping noise interrupts her. "Do you have a celebration of some kind going on?"

Another loud pop is closely followed by several short bursts, and James is on his feet moving for the door. Mr. Von der Slin and his wife are close on his heels. James throws open the door to find several of the pack reverting to their more comfortable forms. Shifting his gaze to Cerita, he tells her, "Get the dagger ready. We're going to need help."

Cerita exchanges concerned expressions with Cercy. "I'm coming."

Cercy quickly ushers her brothers upstairs.

Cerita follows the elf and alpha wolves out the door and into chaos. Several of the wers are coated in fur, and their muscular structure appears to have broadened from earlier in the day. A bright light and loud bang resonates through the air. A howl of rage echoes across the den, with the reverberation penetrating her ears. Her eyes follow the source of the sound to the much larger man standing next to her. Knowing how tall he was with the active microbots only makes him all that more intimidating. The now long hair on the back of the man's neck stands up, and his wife is nearly the same size.

More pops are heard. A whimper, a scream, and the chorus of growls make the events around them clear. Someone has been struck, and the pack is ready to return the attack.

James clears the porch railing and hits the ground at speeds she's never seen. Before she can acknowledge it, he's coated in a similar armor she recalls the knight wearing before. His is sleeker, and cut to his taller, slender form. Without a helmet at the top, he whisks through the pack.

Cerita tries to catch him, only to find herself caught in the rush of bodies moving toward the source of the chaos.

On the edge of the tree line are eight men armed with assorted weapons. One is firing a semi-automatic, long gun into the rushing pack. Another man stands over a large, square device, working on an unidentifiable aspect of it. The rest throw flash-bang grenades and unleash gun fire.

Several of the wers are struck within seconds of the weapons fire starting. As the Von der Slins emerge in front of the pack, the men all train their guns on Mr. Von der Slin. Without a thought, Cerita puts herself between the wolf and humans attacking. She draws her dagger and yells as loudly as possible over the chaos. "Stop this!"

One man lifts his hand and closes it into a fist. The others cease firing and he addresses her. "What are you doing with these abominations?"

"The only abominations I see are the ones standing with weapons and firing upon innocent people." The dagger seems to shift in her hand, but she remains outwardly unfazed.

James stands to her side. Secured to his arm is a small metal crossbow aimed at the lead human. "That's Hines. He's the one I mentioned earlier. The one the lead hunter has to keep under control."

"Ah yes, Elf. I remember you. Didn't you make sure we had a diversion tonight?" The man laughs and points his weapon at James' head.

The alpha male growls.

James shakes his head. "You're attacking while your leader is negotiating with the protector?"

"We just let them think they were negotiating. No one's going to keep these beasts under control, so we're going to stop them here and now." Before he can pull the trigger, the gun is knocked from his hand by a blunt bolt from James' crossbow.

"You don't belong here!" Cerita shouts.

"Why not, girl? Who's going to stop us? Them? These animals can't stop us. They will die like all others who would stalk our kind." The man shakes his hand out as he talks.

Cerita feels her muscles strain to be still. Her mind visualizes her fist impacting the man's face, and the dagger in his gut. As she wretches the dagger from his soft abdomen, coated in his blood, her eyes grow wide. She swallows hard. "You may not attack peaceful people."

The man places both hands over his wound.

Blood pours out around it. His friends move to grab her, but she finds two knocked out by impact wounds delivered by the bowman, and her would be guide, next to her.

On his way down, one of the men finds a handful of Cerita's hair, yanking her with him. The alpha female is upon the man quickly. She pins him to the ground, snarling and angry. Her larger arms and furry hands hold him tightly.

Cerita wiggles free of the human hunter's grasp, and realizes what Mrs. Von der Slin is doing. She puts her hand on the woman's arm. "Please, release him."

"He would kill our young, and you," she snarls.

"If he dies, we're just like them." Cerita blinks as her words sink in and the woman releases the man with bruises forming where he was held. "Thank you."

Another man urges a retreat. The one still working on the large unidentifiable device, slams his hand down on it before he joins his friends. The injured move with limited help from their teammates as the hunters leave the way they came.

A soft wail builds from the device. James covers his ears and drops to his knees as it builds to a higher and louder pitch. Through gritted teeth he explains, "That's an explosive."

Cerita looks around, finding the wers also cowering from the noise. She looks at the device, uncertain what she can do. There is no clear counter. The cube-shaped device is encased in a solid gray shell with speakers on each side. The louder the wail gets, the more vibration she can see in each speaker.

She uses the dagger to begin tearing into one of the speakers. As the wail quiets from the speaker being torn apart, she tears into another, working faster this time, and then another until it's silenced.

As she finishes shredding the last speaker, one of the werwolves stands over the device. Within moments, he opens the case and begins shredding the interior wires. Beads of sweat stream down the man's face. "Space portal!"

Her eyes grow wide. "Portal?"

Suddenly, her dagger begins to glow. A single stream of light is emitted from it, and a circular shimmering window appears to open from that light. The wolf lifts the device and throws it into the window. Before the dagger closes it, a loud noise resonates against the boundary causing the ground to quake enough to knock Cerita off-balance. Her attempts to right herself result in tumbling to the ground.

James is at her side before she can stand on her own. Once on her feet again, she looks around to see the wounded being treated by the pack. "Everyone going to be okay?"

"I think so. It'll be a few days to recover, but I think so." He shakes his head. "I can't believe it."

"What?"

"I can't believe I was deceived like that." He runs a hand through his hair. "I need to get a hold of the master knight."

He steps swiftly to the alpha family. While waiting on Cerita to cover the same distance, James determines that they are unscathed. He leads Cerita around the outside of the large house and opens a private communication channel with the master knight.

The man greets them gruffly. "You're interrupting a very productive meeting."

Before James can respond, Cerita does, with heated anger evident in her tone. "Tell him his plan didn't work. The pack is stronger than ever, and they have protectors."

"First of all, what is she doing there? Second of all, what is she talking about, James?"

"Master Knight, we just fended off an attack from the hunters. They left a makeshift fire bomb that she ported out of here." James' darts his eyes to Cerita. "She's here under the suggestion of her guide."

"You're sure it's the same hunters who attacked the pack?"

"Yes, Master Knight." He sighs. "I'm sure."

"Understood. I expect to see you both at the training facility in the morning."

In unison they respond, "Yes, sir."

James looks at her as the connection closes. "We should assess the pack, and head back home.

We both need to clean up and get some rest before meeting with the master knight in the morning."

Together they go from one family to the next finding out what is needed, and how each one is faring. As the night grows late, the alpha family bids their guests goodbye.

Just before midnight, James pulls into her driveway. "I'll be here after breakfast tomorrow. What time do you normally get up?"

"If I get to sleep at all, I'm not rolling out of bed before the sun, if that's what you mean, farmer."

A huff comes from the elf. "Right. What time?"

"Three?"

"I'll be here by ten."

"Make it eleven, so I can explain to Mother."

"What are you going to tell her? That you fought off humans and used advanced wormhole technology to transport a bomb to protect a werwolf pack?"

"Good point." Her eyes drop to her lap. "I'll think of something."

"I'll see you tomorrow." He fixes his eyes forward as exhaustion starts to settle in.

"Tomorrow." She makes her way into the house, and collapses on her bed within minutes.

** *** **

The sun rises. Carolina wanders into Cerita's bedroom. The toddler crawls to her sister's bed and pulls herself up. With a little effort, she wiggles her way into her sister's slumbering position. Only a few minutes of petting her sister's face pass before the toddler falls asleep again.

** *** **

Cerita wakes late in the morning to find her sister curled up in her arms. She kisses the toddler's forehead. "Did you have breakfast?"

Carolina wakes as her little blue eyes dance in the sunlight. "Sissy."

Cerita wraps her arms around the little girl and carries her into the kitchen. Her mother is serving breakfast, and the boys are washing their plates. "Morning."

Her mother gives her a stern look. "It was late."

"Sorry, Mama. I didn't watch the time." Cerita's eyes drop to the floor.

"Don't make it a habit."

"I won't, Mama."

"Good." Her mother places a plate full of warm pancakes on the table in front of her. "Eat while it's hot." Her warm eyes dance as her daughters settle into a seat together.

A knock at the door leads to Carlos opening it. "Mama, it's Cerita's *boyfriend*."

Her mother's eyes lift and a smile grows as she turns back to the stove to make more breakfast. "Send him back, Carlos. He should eat before they start their day."

Cerita's face turns dark red. Her pulse beats loudly in her ears as James enters the kitchen, with a sweatband covering his ear tips. "I didn't expect you until ten or eleven."

"Oh, you're early. This is good." Her mother turns around with a fresh plate full of pancakes. "Please, join us."

"Mother said I should bring these to you." He extends a small bouquet of wild flowers.

"What great manners, too." Mama turns to Cerita and winks. "I like this boy."

Inwardly, Cerita groans again. "He's alright. But he's *not* my boyfriend."

James confirms, "Nope. I'm helping to train her in self-defense stuff, if that's alright with you."

"As long as you don't bring her in past midnight again, that's fine with me."

"Of course. Time got away from us. I apologize for that." He accepts the plate and sits next to Cerita at the table. "Thank you."

"You're quite welcome." Her mother sits at the table and sips on juice. "So, what kind of training is this?"

Cerita stifles a yawn, puts down her fork, and faces her mother before she responds. "It's something from Europe. I forget what it's called."

"Actually, it's a blend of styles. One from Israel, called Krav Maga. Another is from Ancient Japan." James goes on to explain the class focuses on being able to quickly subdue an attacker, which would give her daughter time to get away from difficult situations.

While he speaks with her mother, Cerita finishes her breakfast. "If you'll excuse me, I need to shower and prepare to meet with the master."

James stands. "Of course."

Her mother pats the table across from her, where he was seated. "I will keep the nice young man company while you prepare, dear."

"Thanks, Mama." She sighs and rushes through the morning prep. Before long, Cerita and James are in his car again, heading to meet with the master knight. As he is parking, she sighs loudly. "Why were you so early?"

"I honestly don't know. Master Knight urged that we got here very early. He actually contacted me in the middle of sleep, aware we had barely been to bed."

"Okay. I guess it's gotta be important then, right?"

James nods, finishes parking, and turns to her. "Know you did very well last night. It was a long night, and only the first of many to come. You adapted better than I expected you would."

"What did you expect?"

"Honestly?"

She nods.

"A bit more disbelief, a lot of screaming, and not a lick of fighting."

She laughs. "Guess you don't know me very well, do you?"

He grins. "I'm happy to say I don't. I'm also happy to say I'm looking forward to changing that."

She opens the car door, but he makes it to the door of the training facility before her. Upon entering, they find the master knight standing with his sword on the ground, and his back to them. The pair exchange looks.

"On the mat. Kneel."

James takes a hold of her elbow and pulls her to the mat, then settles on his knees. She follows. Both remain silent.

"What did you think you were doing last night, James?"

"I am the Knight's Guide. I was guiding my knight to the right choice."

"Were you? She refused. What right did you have to take her into a dangerous situation unprepared?"

"Respectfully, Master Knight, it wasn't expected to be dangerous."

"Your actions were not approved. Neither of you are ready for this."

"What do you mean? We did very well." Cerita's tone is sharp.

"Very well for a couple of ill-prepared children." He turns slowly, with his eyes narrowed. "One man was injured gravely by your dagger. Another sapien hunter out looking for deer saw your wormhole generation. We have damage control teams that have been sent from Atlantis to address the situation. This should never happen on any knight's watch, let alone mine."

Cerita stands, squares herself against the knight and lowers her tone. "It didn't happen on your watch. It happened on *mine*."

He stares into her eyes with fire brimming. "You think you're ready to be a knight?"

"I proved it last night."

He lifts his sword high, and even in his aged form, it moves fluidly. She steps backward. He brings it down over her stopping an inch from her forehead. "You are not the knight."

With a softer tone, she asks, "Then what are you expecting if I am not a knight?"

"Your mantle might become Knight's Apprentice. You must earn the title of Knight through training you have not begun." He pulls the sword back and then spins it in his hands until the blade is pointed down, bringing it to her abdomen, without making contact. "You will *never* speak on my behalf without my permission. Do you understand?"

Her eyes drift to the blade that touches her shirt, but not her body. "Yes."

"You will never move into a dangerous situation without preparation. Understood?"

"Yes."

"You will address this with the utmost sincerity. People's lives will depend on you. Children will need you to make choices that allow them to continue. I won't have someone who will run from the duties, thus risking lives." He lowers the sword but does not put it down.

"I won't."

"Why should I believe that?"

"Because I witnessed men trying to kill children, families, for no reason at all. Because I can't stand crap against people in school, let alone with the people I met last night. Because I understand it to be the job of the knights to stop that."

He pauses. He stares at her intently before finally placing the tip of his blade on the ground again. "Prepare for the fiercest training you will ever encounter. You will maintain your grades, your appearance to the homo-sapien world, and you will comply with *all* of my orders. Do I make myself clear?"

"Yes." She swallows hard, pauses, then adds, "Sir."

He sheaths the sword without taking his eyes off of her. "Good. You have one month before the Choosing. We will know then, if you're going to become a knight."

"When do we start?" She steps back from her master knight.

"Now."

Knight's Apprentice

Sneak Peak of the next book

The Choosing

In the car, Cerita pulls the ball from her bag again, and stares at it. The light grows brighter the longer she holds it.

James notices the glow and it draws his attention enough that he pulls over to the side of the road. "Where did you get that?"

With her eyes wide, Cerita looks at him, "Mom gave it to me. Said something about Daddy having it set aside for me. You know what it is?"

"I know what it looks like, but I've never seen one in person. The orb, if it's an orb, would represent one of the founding families. There are only twelve." James stares at it as it glows in her hand. "May I?"

She shrugs and passes it to him. When it's resting in his hand, the light goes out. "Hmm."

His eyes look at the blue color and then back to her. "Don't show this to the master knight. After the council tonight, I want to ask Aunt Vivian if it's what I think it is."

She shrugs and nods. "Okay."

He passes the ball back to her and it glows

again. With focused intent, he carefully pulls back onto the road and moves toward the training gym. This time, his mind is distracted by the implications that could apply to a hybrid of a family of such rank.

When he parks, she tucks the ball back in her bag, and secures it. James opens the door for her and they enter the gym, lock the door, and draw the front blinds.

Master Knight Frederickson is waiting for them. Once they stand near him with their bags over their shoulders, he gives them a look over, top to bottom. With a heavy sigh, he extends his arm to her shoulder. "Cerita Guzman, when we step through that portal, you'll find yourself in a city unlike anything you've ever known. The buildings are tall, and the city is spread wide. But what is most important for you to remember is your manners. You are the outsider, but you belong there as much as the next person. Give some the impression you don't . . . well, just don't give them that impression."

"Okay. When will we meet with Jenna?"

The older gentleman half smiles. "Anxious?"

She rubs her hands together. "Yeah. I think. Just a little bit."

James smiles broadly. "Well, I think you're going to enjoy what you see. I'm looking forward to showing you the city."

The knight shoots him a warning expression. "With Jenna?"

"Of course." He looks around. "Why isn't she coming from the same point?"

"She left hours ago. This portal is being sent for us specifically. We'll meet with the council members overseeing the Choosing and then we'll be free for the evening."

He grumbles, "Unless you're an elf. Then you have to face the council for their approval to participate in the Choosing." He shakes his head. Years of training could disappear in a single gesture from the triad council. The thought sends tingles down his spine in the worst possible way.

Suddenly, a bright light appears in the wall ahead of them. First it is yellow, then it shifts to a soft blue, and then a purple spiral twists within the blue.

"It's steady." James mutters before securing his wrist mounted crossbow on his arm. "Ready?"

Cerita nods.

The master knight steps forward into the portal first with his sword in hand.

Cerita takes the lead of her master and guide by securing her dagger to her hip before hesitantly stepping toward the portal. Stopping short of the event horizon, she turns toward James. "Just step in?"

He smiles at her. "Yes, my knight. Just step in."

Her eyes linger on his longer than her mind justifies. She takes a deep breath and steps forward into the purple spiral. A strange sensation overwhelms her senses. Her skin experiences a cold tingling rush. When she crosses into the event horizon all sound stops. She's unable to hear even the sound of her own heartbeat. Her eyes are overwhelmed by the purple spiral for several minutes. The faintest smell of baby powder seems to float around her. Suddenly, as if hit by a rush of wind and fresh air, her lungs fill. She can feel solid ground beneath her feet again. She blinks, and blinks again. Her eyes adjust to the new level of light. The master knight, in full armor, stands at her left. To her right steps James, and in front of her are three individuals.

One resembles the elfin woman she knows to be James' aunt. The other two stand just behind her. To her right is a taller man with long hair to his shoulders. It's dark, almost black in color. His features are human, leading her to believe he is homo-supreme, like she is. To the left is a darker complected gentleman with deep colored fur that coats his body behind the suit he wears.

Cerita watches those around her for an idea of what to do next.

Master Knight Frederickson speaks first. "Hello, council members. May I introduce, James, the Knight's Guide in training, and Cerita, my Apprentice in training." He gestures to Cerita. "Cerita, this is Councilwoman Vivian Sáralondë, Councilman Ral Shola, and Councilman Clayton Blocc. They will oversee the Choosing."

She smiles slightly, acknowledges each one in turn, and awaits instructions.

James steps forward and speaks in a language Cerita's unfamiliar with. His aunt responds in kind. Knight Frederickson turns his eyes to his apprentice and adds to the conversation in the foreign tongue. Councilman Ral answers what sounds like a question from Councilwoman Sáralondë. At this point, Councilman Blocc clears his throat. The group becomes quiet.

"Not all participants speak the familiar language of the Elves." The councilman steps forward. "She is merely an apprentice in training. Language is a later developed skill, although with an elven guide, she will likely come to know the language rapidly, as the need arises."

Councilman Ral Shola nods. "You are correct, my old friend. I shall recall my manners."

The councilwoman remains emotionless in tone, features, and sound.

Councilman Blocc pats his friend on the shoulder. "Shola, it is easy to be drawn into common practices." His attention turns to the apprentices. "You are the last to arrive. Are your arrangements finalized?"

James responds first. "I will be with my order." He lowers his head in the direction of his aunt. "Tonight, there will be an Elven Calling."

Vivian nods but says nothing.

"And you, Cerita?" Councilman Blocc's tone seems to peak in interest.

"I am staying with a friend in the city."

"Good. Master Knight?"

"My home is available within the confines of the Knight's Realm. I will be there when we are not training."

Councilwoman Sáralondë inquires, "They are not prepared, under your guidance, prior to the Choosing?"

"My pupil has had a month to prepare, at the council's behest. She is prepared for any competition you may present to her. However, expanding knowledge is a never ending quest, especially for one at the beginning of their journey." The master knight crosses his arms.

Cerita's eyes divert to the armor and away from the scrutiny of those of the council.

The elf woman does not respond further.

"Presentation will be at sunrise. A short break will follow and then the beginning of the Choosing commences. You will be forced into a variety of competition. Some will not be of this world, nor the world from which you come." Councilman Ral gestures to the dome above.

For the first time, Cerita's eyes dare to look up. Although the ceiling of the city appears to be far above, she can still see large sea creatures swimming not far from the dome shape. Her eyes grow big, her mouth opens slightly, and she stares as a large, blue whale almost touches the surface with its tail.

Councilman Blocc laughs. "Yes, it is quite a

sight to behold."

"Do they ever . . ."

James places his hand on her shoulder briefly. "No. The dome is solid, and flexible. Nothing gets in that isn't permitted."

Ral Shola adds, "Not through the dome they do not."

Councilman Blocc and Councilwoman Sáralondë both give him side glances. He clears his throat. "We will see you at sunrise."

The council members begin to depart, leading the newest arrivals to a doorway a fair distance from the arrival point. Councilman Blocc slows his pace until he is next to Cerita. He leans over and whispers, "Pay no attention to her tone. She's been quite warm to you."

Cerita mumbles, "I don't ever want to be on her bad side if this is warm."

He chuckles. "No one wants to be on her bad side. She's got a way with things that can surprise anyone. Comes with age."

Cerita smiles a little.

"Are you going with your guide to the Elven Calling?"

She shrugs. "I'm not sure yet. I think I'm expected."

"Has anyone explained the Calling to you?"

She shrugs again. "Kinda. James said he'll meet with the council of elven elders and they'll decide if we will continue."

Councilman Blocc nods. "That's the short

version. The full story is that they are measuring him. They will determine if he meets the standards expected of an elf in such an important position."

Cerita slows her steps. "How?"

"I'm uncertain. In my many years of life, I have never been invited inside the Calling, even as a witness. It's a very special privilege that you have been."

"My guide is the elf in question."

"And this is also a privilege. You have many for someone coming from among the mainland humans." He smiles. "If things ever get tough, remember you're a knight. Pay no mind to anything else during this process. Know you're worthy of anything they wish to question. Keep that in mind and there is no challenge you will face in this city, or anywhere, that will hold you back."

"Thank you for your confidence. I wish I felt as strongly as you do about that."

"You are here because you come from a race full of strength and pride who, like you, seek to do what is right for everyone. You're going to be great." He puts his hand on her shoulder. "When this is over, you and your guide will come to my home and we'll celebrate with a feast."

"May I ask a question?"

"Of course."

"How many knight positions need to be secured during this choosing?"

"We have three planets, counting Earth, that will need skills like yours." His tone becomes business again.

"How many of us are competing?"

"There are five teams with one knight and one guide. Each team will face different challenges. Most are catered to their unique limitations." The councilman's brow furrows. "Did your master not explain this to you?"

"I'm aware of how the challenges should be difficult. I'm aware things were limited, but I'm grateful you told me how many knights were needed." She kicks the ground with her eyes lowered.

"You're worried?"

"I know I can be assigned offworld," her face slightly lightens with the hint of a smile, "once I'm selected." Her eyes lift again to meet his. "There are some other concerns should that occur."

"No matter where you're assigned, you still have years ahead of you as an apprentice." His face softens. "You'll be able to get things in order on Earth if you're assigned offworld."

"May I ask why, if there is a Knight of Earth already, does the council need another?"

The councilman lifts his finger, and half smiles. "That, young one, is something you will have to ask your master, in time. For now, we should catch up with them so you can get to the Calling, and a good night's rest."

From the Author:

Thank you for starting this new journey with me and the cast of characters that make up the Knights of the Immortals Series. Already in some stage of preparation are the first six books of the series. This is a thrilling adventure that'll take us off world, into new communities, and adventures yet unseen.

Please, don't hesitate to leave a message for me at the <u>Knights of the Immortals Facebook Page</u> or on twitter @TheLadyWrites

As thank you to my fantastic fans and reviewers, watch for your name to appear as one of the many upcoming characters in the series. I often pick character names from those generous enough to leave reviews. Can't wait to share where this journey leads!

Watch for books two through six.

Have fun!

See you for the next book!

Catrina Taylor
Author of Xarrok & Knights of the Immortals

Join the discussion on facebook in the Xarrok Group or on the Knight's Page.

Catrina Taylor

www.ingramcontent.com/pod-product-compliance
Lightning Source LLC
Chambersburg PA
CBHW020323130626
46549CB00003B/995